Kira Bigwood

SECRET, SECRET AGENT GUY

Illustrated by Celia Krampien

A lullaby for little spies set to the tune of "Twinkle, Twinkle, Little Star"

 Atheneum Books for Young Readers New York   London   Toronto   Sydney   New Delhi

Secret, secret agent guy, working for the FBI.

On a mission
from the top:

Get your gear on—
first things first—

pausing just to quench your thirst.

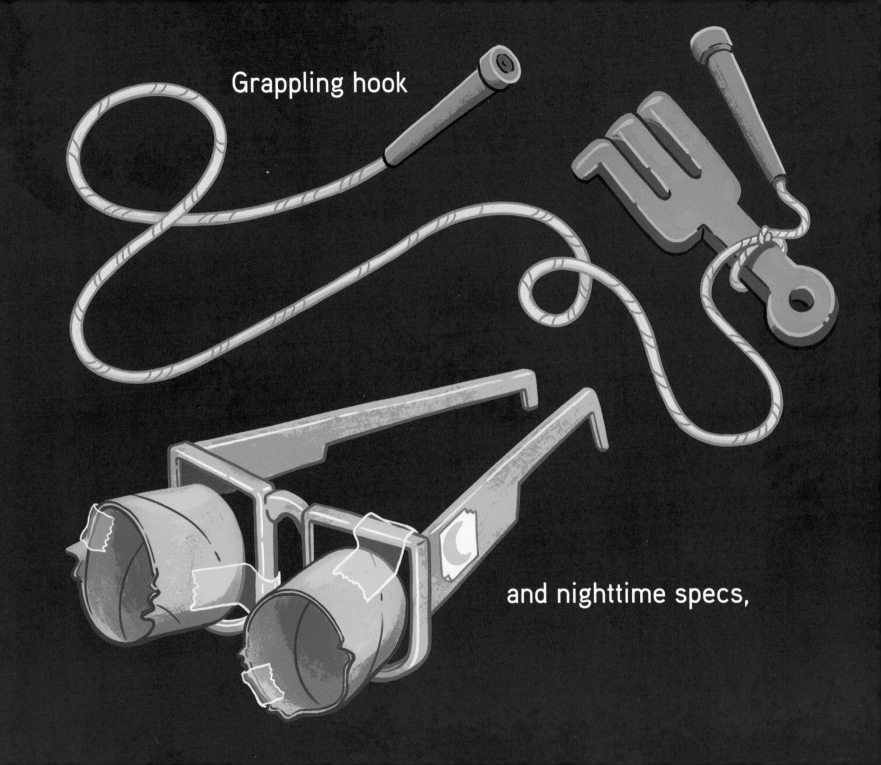

Grappling hook

and nighttime specs,

walkie-talkies,

check
check
check!

Sneak downstairs, survey the scene,

boss is calling
on your screen.

Set your traps and get to work;
in the shadows something lurks.

Mom and Dad have sent a spy.

Lucky that he's on your side.

Careful now,
you're almost there.

Grab the handle,

snatch with care.

Take a breath

and get a grip.

Grab that jet pack,
let 'er rip.

Someone's waiting
at the drop.

Off they whisk
the mother lode—

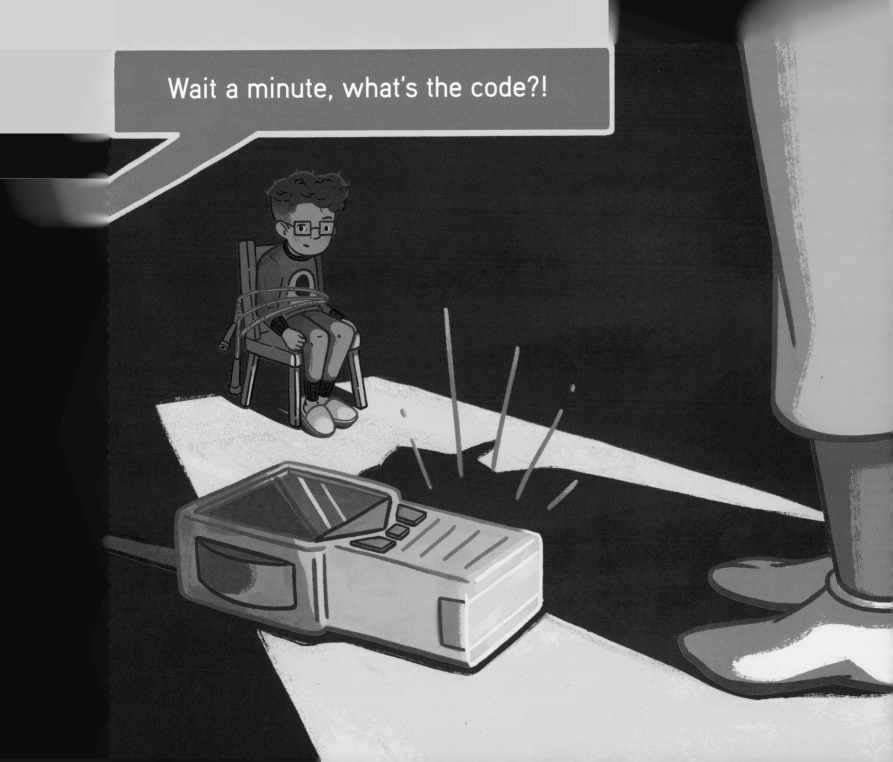

Turns out you've been double-crossed.

Both you
and your boss
got bossed.

Secret, secret
agent girl—

first, to bed,
then save
the world.

To Agent G., Agent T., and Agent H., with love
—K. B.

For Jamie. Thank you.
—C. K.

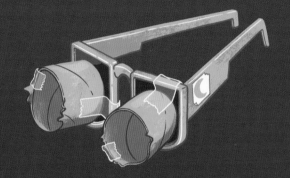

ATHENEUM BOOKS FOR YOUNG READERS
An imprint of Simon & Schuster Children's Publishing Division
1230 Avenue of the Americas, New York, New York 10020
Text © 2021 by Kira Bigwood
Illustrations © 2021 by Celia Krampien
Book design by Lauren Rille © 2021 by Simon & Schuster, Inc.
All rights reserved, including the right of reproduction in whole or in part in any form.
ATHENEUM BOOKS FOR YOUNG READERS is a registered trademark of Simon & Schuster, Inc.
Atheneum logo is a trademark of Simon & Schuster, Inc.
For information about special discounts for bulk purchases, please contact Simon & Schuster Special Sales
at 1-866-506-1949 or business@simonandschuster.com.
The Simon & Schuster Speakers Bureau can bring authors to your live event. For more information or to book an event,
contact the Simon & Schuster Speakers Bureau at 1-866-248-3049 or visit our website at www.simonspeakers.com.
The text for this book was set in Aaux.
The illustrations for this book were digitally rendered.
Manufactured in China
0321 SCP
10 9 8 7 6 5 4 3 2
Library of Congress Cataloging-in-Publication Data
Names: Bigwood, Kira, author. | Krampien, Celia, 1988– illustrator.
Title: Secret, secret agent guy / Kira Bigwood ; illustrated by Celia Krampien.
Description: First edition. | New York : Atheneum Books for Young Readers, [2021] | Audience: Ages 4–8. | Audience:
Grades K–1. | Summary: "When a 007-year-old embarks on a bedtime mission called Operation Lollipop, he's prepared for
every eventuality—except one"—Provided by publisher.
Identifiers: LCCN 2019056295 (print) | LCCN 2019056296 (eBook) | ISBN 9781534469211 (hardcover) |
ISBN 9781534469228 (eBook)
Subjects: CYAC: Stories in rhyme. | Spies—Fiction. | Bedtime—Fiction.
Classification: LCC PZ8.3.B487 Se 2021 (print) | LCC PZ8.3.B487 (eBook) | DDC [E]—dc23
LC record available at https://lccn.loc.gov/2019056295
LC eBook record available at https://lccn.loc.gov/2019056296